Wishes really do come true

Lucky Stars

Lucky Star that shines so bright,
Who will need your help tonight?
Light up the sky, it's thanks to you
Wishes really do come true . . .

Lucky Stars

The Best Friend Wish

The Perfect Pony Wish

The Pop Singer Wish

The Birthday Wish

The Film Star Wish

The Ballerina Wish

Explore the sparkling world of the stars at

www.luckystarsbooks.co.uk

Wishes really do come true

Lucky Stars

The Best Friend Wish

Phoebe Bright

Illustrated by Karen Donnelly

MACMILLAN CHILDREN'S BOOKS

A Working Partners book

Special thanks to Valerie Wilding

First published 2012 by Macmillan Children's Books
a division of Macmillan Publishers Limited
20 New Wharf Road, London N1 9RR
Basingstoke and Oxford
Associated companies throughout the world
www.panmacmillan.com

ISBN 978-1-4472-0233-2

3 5 7 9 8 6 4

A CIP catalogue record for this book is available from
the British Library.

Printed and bound by CPI Group (UK) Ltd, Croydon CR0 4YY

For Elsie Beard, with all my love

Contents

Hello, friend!

I'm Stella Starkeeper and I want to tell you a secret. Have you ever gazed up at the stars and thought how magical they looked? Well, you're right. Stars really do have magic!

Their precious glittering light allows me to fly down from the sky, all the way to Earth. You see, I'm always on the lookout for boys and girls who are especially kind and helpful. I train them to become Lucky Stars - people who can make wishes come true!

So the next time you're under the twinkling night sky, look out for me. I'll be floating among the stars somewhere. Do give me a wave!

Love from
Stella x

1
The Silver Tent

'Whee!' cried Cassie.

'Whoa!' shouted her mum.

The spinning-teacup ride whirled so fast that the blue of the sea and sky blurred into the bright fairground colours.

When the ride stopped, Cassie heard Mum take a deep shaky breath.

She giggled. 'We'll try something slower next,' Cassie said. She felt a bit dizzy herself.

Mum tottered out of the teacup. 'It's your birthday, my lucky star,' she said. 'Choose whatever you like.'

Cassie thought how lucky she was to live in Astral-on-Sea. Her cliff-top home, Starwatcher Towers, overlooked the whole

town and the beach. Even though she had
no brothers or sisters to play with, there
was so much to do – exploring rock pools,
shell-collecting, building sandcastles . . . And
now the funfair had arrived!

'Helter-skelter?' asked Mum. 'Or bumper
cars?'

Cassie couldn't decide. Then she
spotted a small tent, glistening silver in the
sunshine. A sequinned curtain covered the
entrance, with a sign above, saying:

Lucky Dip!

'What's a lucky dip?' she asked.

'A box of surprises,' said Mum. 'You
close your eyes, put your hand inside and
pull out a gift.'

'I like the sound of that!' said Cassie.

7

As they reached the tent, she noticed a small bell next to the entrance with a rope of silvery stars dangling from it. She peered round the curtain. A woman in a long cloak was sitting behind a large wooden box.

Cassie had the oddest feeling that she simply must enter the silver tent. She turned to Mum. 'Can I go in, please?'

'A lucky dip for a lucky star!' said Mum. She took a coin from her purse. 'Give this to the lady. I'll wait here.'

Cassie slipped the coin into her pocket. Gently, she pulled the rope of stars and jangled the bell.

'Come in,' called the woman in a soft, clear voice.

Lucky Stars

Cassie's tummy fluttered as she drew back the sequinned curtain. Inside, the tent was softly lit by clusters of glass baubles that dangled on sparkling threads. They were shaped like stars and moons and planets.

'They're so pretty,' breathed Cassie. 'My bedroom's got a glass ceiling, and your baubles remind me of the stars I can see through it. I live in an observatory,' she explained. 'I'm even named after the stars.'

The woman smiled. 'Cassiopeia is my favourite constellation,' she said.

Cassie stared. 'That's my name!' she said. 'How did you know?'

'A lucky guess?' said the woman. Her cloak was the colour of moonlit sky, and a matching scarf was draped over her head and face. A lock of silver-blonde hair rippled across her shoulder.

Cassie sat in the chair opposite. Now she could make out the woman's eyes. They were a deep velvety-blue, and sparkled like stars.

'Happy birthday,' the woman said in her soft voice. 'Seven is a very special age, you know.'

Cassie's mouth fell open in surprise. 'How do you know it's my birthday? And how do you know I'm seven?' she asked. 'You must be very good at guessing.'

'Perhaps,' the woman said. Her eyes sparkled brightly. 'Look.'

She lifted the lid of her box. It was full of

tiny silver stars, twinkling like fairy lights.

Cassie gasped.

'Many things are hidden among these stars,' the woman said. 'One of them is yours. Can you find it?'

Cassie dipped into the box. The stars rustled as she searched among them. Her fingers closed over something solid, and a shivery feeling passed up her arm.

This must be it, she thought, and pulled out a delicate silver chain.

'Wonderful! I knew you'd find your bracelet,' said the woman.

'*My* bracelet? What do you mean?' Cassie asked. 'I've never seen it before.'

The woman fastened the chain on to Cassie's wrist. 'You'll find out before your birthday is over,' she said. 'And now you must go.'

Cassie stroked the cool, shiny surface of the bracelet. 'I love it,' she said. 'Thank you very much. Goodbye.'

'Goodbye,' said the woman, 'for now . . .'

Outside in the sunshine, Cassie showed her mum the bracelet.

'That was good value,' said Mum. 'Are you sure she meant you to keep it?'

'Yes,' said Cassie. 'She says it's mine.'

There was a sudden squeal from the beach. A donkey was nibbling at a woman's deckchair, and she was flapping her towel at it.

'Look!' Cassie cried. 'Bert needs help.'

Bert had six donkeys for children to ride on the beach. One of them, Coco, had wandered away. Cassie ran across the sand and gave him a hug. He was new, and a little nervous, but he was getting braver every day.

'You'll soon be best friends with the other donkeys, Coco,' Cassie whispered as she led him back to the others.

Bert's wrinkled brown face broke into a grin. 'Thanks, Cassie,' he said, 'and happy birthday!'

'Thank you!' Cassie waved goodbye as she ran back.

The Best Friend Wish

'It's time for some birthday cake now,' Mum said, 'then I must get ready for the new guests.'

Part of Starwatcher Towers was Mum's

B & B. Dad worked in the other part,
which was the observatory. His job was to
study the stars and planets. Today, though,
he was in the kitchen, icing Cassie's
birthday cake in secret. Every year he
decorated it differently.

The Best Friend Wish

Something fell from Cassie's pocket and plopped into the sand. It was the coin Mum had given her for the woman in the silver tent. 'Oh no! I forgot to pay,' she said.

'Let's take it to her on our way home,' said Mum.

But later, however hard they looked, they couldn't find the little silver tent anywhere. *It's completely vanished*, thought Cassie. *Like magic.*

While Mum settled the new guests in their rooms, Cassie had a last sliver of cake. This year Dad had iced it with a shower of shooting stars in different colours.

'It's not what stars really look like,' he said, 'but it's pretty.'

Lucky Stars

'It's gorgeous!' Cassie and Mum said together.

At bedtime, Cassie took her presents upstairs. Twinkle, her old cat, was already snoozing on the pillow.

Cassie loved her room. The B & B had two domes for viewing the sky, and her bedroom was inside the smaller one. It was almost completely round and half of the roof was made from glass panels. On clear nights Cassie would lie in bed and gaze at the stars. With her moon-shaped nightlight casting a soft glow over the starry wallpaper, and with real stars above, Cassie liked to imagine she was drifting through the sky. When it rained, it was like being beneath a waterfall without getting wet!

Once Cassie was in her purple star pyjamas, she went to take her bracelet off.

No, she decided. *I'll keep it on. It will remind me of my lovely day.*

Cassie jumped into bed, then leaned over and thumped twice on the floor to tell Mum and Dad she was ready. When they came in, Mum told her that the new guests had a son her age. 'You'll see him tomorrow,' she promised.

Cassie kissed Dad goodnight. 'Thank you for a lovely birthday and the yummy cake.'

Just as Mum kissed her, Dad gave a shout, making them all jump.

'Look!' he cried, pointing through the glass ceiling. 'A meteor shower!'

Cassie scrambled upright. 'Wow!' she said. The sky was filled with streaks of light. She knew they were really meteors – glowing trails left by bits of space dust or rocks – but she preferred to call them shooting stars. After all, that's what they looked like! As she watched them flash against the darkness, she felt a tingle of excitement.

'How strange,' said Mum. 'There was a

The Best Friend Wish

meteor shower like this the night you were
born, Cassie.'

Dad rubbed his hands together. 'Forget

21

bed! Let's go to the observatory and watch it through my telescopes,' he said.

Cassie usually jumped at the chance to look through Dad's telescopes, but tonight, for some reason, she wanted to watch the shooting stars by herself and feel the cool night breeze on her face. 'I'll look from here,' she said. 'Dad – can you open one of the panels, please?'

He turned a lever so that a section of the glass ceiling swung open, then hurried out of the room with Mum.

The shooting stars reminded Cassie of the glass baubles in the silver tent. She glanced down at her bracelet, and what she saw made her gasp. It was fizzing with tiny silver sparkles!

The Best Friend Wish

'Wow! Why's it doing that, Twinkle?' she asked her cuddly old cat.

But Twinkle was staring upward. His fur went bristly and his tail flicked. Suddenly he yowled, leapt off the bed and dived beneath it.

Cassie looked up to see what had scared

him. One shooting star, bigger than the
rest, was swirling downward. Closer and
closer it came.

And it seemed to be heading straight for
Cassie!

2
Stella Starkeeper

With a *whizz* and a *fizz* and a *zip-zip-zip*,
the star shot through the open glass panel,
showering silver sparkles around the room.

Cassie was so astonished she couldn't
move. What was happening?

The star slowed and hovered just above
the rug. Cassie stared as it grew into a
column of dazzling light, which slowly
changed into a lovely young woman,
dressed all in silver. She wore a shiny

cropped jacket with star-shaped buttons on the cuffs. Her short silky dress rippled above glittery leggings and shiny boots. In her hand was a wand, tipped with a twinkling star.

The Best Friend Wish

The woman's crown was woven from delicate strands of silver, and her fair hair shone like a silver river. As she smiled, her velvety-blue eyes sparkled.

Cassie had seen those eyes before. 'You gave me the bracelet!' she cried.

'I did,' said the woman in her soft voice. 'My name is Stella Starkeeper. And who's this?'

Twinkle had crept out from under the bed. As Stella tickled his chin, Cassie noticed that she wore a bracelet like her own, but with charms on it.

The old cat purred, and patted the wand with his paw. A shower of silver glitter floated to the rug.

'Is this about my bracelet?' Cassie

asked. 'Is it magical?'

Stella took her hand. 'It is,' she said.
'Now, would you like to see some more
magic?'

Cassie nodded and with a *whoosh* found
herself flying up through the open window
with Stella. 'Oh!' she gasped. She felt
as light as a balloon as they circled the
treetops, floating high in the night sky.

Up and up they soared. Cassie felt
her hair streaming behind her. She
looked down and saw a light on in Dad's
observatory. Could he see her through
his telescope? What would he think? The
thought made laughter bubble up inside her.

They left the lights of Astral-on-Sea
far below as Stella took Cassie higher and

higher, until they were flying among the
stars.

'They're all different colours,' Cassie
breathed. 'Violet and gold, orange and
scarlet. And they're playing together!'

The stars danced and bobbed all around
them. Cassie watched a tiny pink star

chase a little blue one in circles. They
reminded her of kittens frisking round a
tree. Suddenly, the pink star skidded and
tumbled towards her.

'The poor thing can't stop,' Cassie cried.
She reached out and gently patted the pink
star back towards its little blue friend.

As the star bobbed around happily once
more, Stella waved her wand.

Cassie felt her wrist tingle. She looked
down to see a tiny bird charm dangling
from her bracelet. Sparkles swirled around
her, and now she tingled all over. Then
she realized that something amazing had
happened. Stella wasn't holding her hand
any more.

'I'm flying!' she cried. 'All by myself!'

For a moment she was afraid, but when Stella smiled she smiled too. With a shiver of excitement, Cassie turned through the air in a forward roll, feeling as free as a bird.

'Am I like you, Stella?' she wondered. 'I can fly now, and I've got a bracelet like yours.'

Stella flew alongside Cassie as they moved among the bright bobbing stars. 'Would you like that?' she asked. 'Would you like to become a *real* Lucky Star?'

'Yes!' Cassie cried. 'But what does that mean?'

'Lucky Stars use their magic to make wishes come true,' said Stella, her pale hair swirling behind her.

Cassie grinned. 'Then I *definitely* want to become a Lucky Star! But how?'

'By being yourself,' said Stella. 'I chose you because you can't resist helping people – like you helped the tiny pink star.' She touched Cassie's bracelet. 'That bird charm is the first step in your Lucky Star training. It gives you the power to fly.'

They swooped away as a bunch of lime green stars danced around their heads.

'To become a Lucky Star, you must be

on the lookout for someone with a wish,'
Stella continued. 'If you make their wish
come true, you'll receive another charm
with a new magical power. When you've
collected seven charms, you'll be a Lucky
Star.' She smiled at Cassie. 'And Lucky Stars
don't have to wait for wishes. They can

grant them whenever they like!'

They floated downward. Cassie could see the sea, glinting in the moonlight. 'Nearly home,' she said as Stella waved her wand. She felt sleepy. Her eyes closed for a moment. 'Nearly... home...'

The Best Friend Wish

When Cassie opened her eyes again, she found herself back in bed. Stella Starkeeper had gone. She snuggled under her quilt and Twinkle settled down beside her.

'I'll be a Lucky Star one day, Twinkle,' she murmured. 'I'm going to do my best to make wishes come true.'

The old cat purred, and Cassie closed her eyes.

'I wonder who I'll help first,' she murmured. 'I can't wait until tomorrow!'

3
Alex and Comet

Sizzle, hiss, sizzle!

'Mmm,' Cassie murmured. She stretched, and sniffed. Bacon! Mum was cooking breakfast.

Cassie quickly washed and dressed, wondering what the new guests were like. She hoped their son was nice.

As she went downstairs, her bracelet jangled against the banister. She remembered her night-time adventure, and

the bird charm. 'I flew!' she said out loud.
'Or was that just a dream?'

No one was about, so Cassie decided to
do a test.

She stood on the bottom stair, squeezed
her eyes shut and thought about her bird
charm.

Instantly, she
felt herself
floating
upward. As
she opened
her eyes,
she saw she
was drifting
gently down
the hallway

towards the kitchen. Sparkles shimmered around her bracelet.

'It was real!' she cried, and floated back down on to the carpet.

Mum popped her head out of the kitchen. 'What was real?'

Cassie hesitated. She didn't think Mum would believe her if she explained about Stella or her new bird charm. She could hardly believe it herself!

'Nothing,' Cassie said at last. She pointed to her old cat, who was settling on his cushion beneath the hall radiator. 'I was talking to Twinkle.'

'Well, go into the dining room and talk to the guests,' said Mum. 'I'm just bringing breakfast through.'

A man, a woman and a boy with curly
brown hair were sitting at the long wooden
table.

'Hello,' said Cassie.

'Hello!' they replied together.

The woman smiled. 'You must be Cassie.

This is our son, Alex,' she said. 'And that's Comet under the table.'

Under the table? Cassie bent down and saw a small fluffy white puppy chewing a blue rubber bone. He wagged his tail.

Twinkle won't like Comet staying here! she thought.

Alex seemed to be concentrating on a box in his lap. Cassie glanced at it, and saw test tubes inside.

'What's that?' she asked.

Alex fidgeted. 'Well, er . . . actually, it's top secret,' he said.

'Show Cassie,' said his dad. 'I'm sure she won't tell anyone.'

'Course not,' said Cassie.

'It's my experiment,' Alex told her. 'I'm

going to be a scientist when I grow up.'

'Are you really?' Cassie was interested. 'What's the experiment for?'

Alex tapped a notebook that lay beside his cereal bowl. 'It's all in here,' he said, 'but it's easier to show you.' He held a test tube over the bowl. 'The white powder in here is bicarbonate of soda, and I'm going to add some of this green food colouring. Can you get me some vinegar, please?'

Cassie fetched the bottle from the sideboard.

'Watch,' said Alex as he poured some into the test tube.

The mixture fizzed and bubbled into a green froth that erupted into the bowl.

'Wow!' said Cassie. 'That's like magic!'

'It's not magic,' said Alex, shrugging his shoulders. 'It's science.' He jotted down some notes. 'These are my observations.'

'You'd get on with my dad,' said Cassie. 'He's an astronomer.'

Alex's father grinned. 'We're on holiday here for two weeks, so I'm sure Alex would love to see Mr Cafferty's observatory.'

Cassie gave Alex a smile, but he just carried on writing in his notebook.

Cassie's mum hurried in with enormous plates of bacon, eggs, sausages, tomatoes and mushrooms, but Cassie decided just to have a piece of toast and leave. Alex didn't seem particularly friendly and, besides, she wanted to see if what Stella Starkeeper had said last night about becoming a Lucky Star was true. It sounded so exciting.

The Best Friend Wish

I wonder who's got a special wish, she thought as she crunched her toast. *And how can I make it come true?*

4
Helping Bert

'Excuse me,' Cassie said to Alex's family. 'I'm going out now.' She reached down to stroke the snuffly little puppy.

'Bye, Comet.'

As she stood up, she
accidentally bumped
the edge of the
table, making the
cups and plates
rattle. 'Oops!'

Two apples toppled from the fruit bowl. Cassie caught one and, just before the other rolled off the table, Alex grabbed it.

He passed it to her. 'Here you go.'

'You moved fast!' said Cassie. 'Thanks.'

He smiled, then quickly looked down. *He's not unfriendly*, thought Cassie suddenly. *He's shy!*

'Would you like to come to the beach?' she asked him.

Alex's face lit up. 'Really?'

48

he gasped. 'Yes, please!' He put his box carefully in the middle of the sideboard. Then he jigged about as if he couldn't wait to get going. 'Can we take Comet?' he asked.

'Yes,' said his dad, 'but don't let him run off.'

'We won't, I promise,' said Cassie.

Alex clipped a lead to Comet's collar and they stepped into the morning sunshine. Cassie noticed Twinkle sunning himself in the garden. But when he spotted the puppy he scuttled under the hedge.

'Yupp! Yupp!' Comet barked. He pulled on his lead, trying to reach the cat.

'He wants to play,' said Alex.

'But he's scaring Twinkle,' said Cassie.

'Don't worry,' she told her cat. 'Comet's just visiting for a while.'

As they walked down the hill towards the beach, Comet struggled ahead. His body moved too quickly for his legs, and he kept tumbling over.

'He's so cute,' said Cassie. 'And quick! Comets are actually just frozen dust and gas, but they travel round the sun at hundreds of miles an hour. So Comet's a good name for him!'

'That's interesting,' said Alex. 'You know lots about stars and planets, don't you?'

Cassie nodded. 'My dad tells me all about them.' She suddenly realized she knew things about stars that her dad didn't know – how they liked to play, for instance. She'd even touched one!

When they reached the part of the beach where dogs were allowed, Cassie and Alex jumped off the low wall on to the warm sand. Comet sniffed the sea air and barked with excitement.

As they wandered along, Cassie looked around, trying to find someone who needed her help. But everybody seemed perfectly content. Couples snoozed in deckchairs. Children dug in the sand, or splashed in the rippling waves. A toddler was crying in the ice-cream queue on the promenade, but his dad was next to be served. He didn't need help.

A woman struggled to push her buggy across the sand. As it jiggled along, a small

blue teddy fell out. Cassie ran to pick up
the teddy and give it back to the baby, who
gurgled his thanks.

Immediately, Cassie checked her bracelet.
The bird charm dangled on its own.

*I suppose the baby wasn't really wishing for
my help*, thought Cassie. *But I'm glad I made
him smile.*

'Yupp! Yupp!' Comet watched Bert's
line of donkeys and riders, way down near
the water's edge.

'Stay!' said Alex. But Comet wanted to
meet the donkeys. He yelped and pulled
and suddenly he was gone, trailing his lead
behind him!

'Quick, after him!' shouted Cassie. 'If he
frightens the donkeys, they'll bolt and the

children
could fall
off.'

The
deep soft
sand made
it difficult to run.

'We won't catch him in time,' panted
Cassie. 'Poor Coco will be so scared!'
Her bracelet jingled as she ran and she
remembered her bird charm. *Oh*, she
thought, *I wonder* . . .

Instantly she tingled all over. Tiny
silvery sparks danced around her bracelet.
Cassie felt herself rise a little so her feet
were just above the sand. She floated
past Alex and caught up with Comet in

an instant, grabbing hold of his lead.

'Got him!' she called.

She saw Alex giving her a strange look. *Flying's my special secret*, Cassie thought. *I'm not ready to tell anyone about it yet.*

Quickly, she curled into a forward roll on the sand, hoping Alex would think she'd just done a spectacular acrobatic move.

Alex picked Comet up and turned to Bert. 'Sorry,' he began, but Bert was gazing at his candyfloss stall on the promenade. He looked hot and bothered.

'What's wrong?' Cassie asked.

'My son should be selling candyfloss today,' said Bert, 'but he's at home with a cold. I'm worn out going from the donkeys to the candyfloss and back again. It's hard to

keep an eye on everything.'

Cassie's heart leapt. It sounded like Bert was wishing for help!

'I'll do it!' she said. 'I'll make the candyfloss.'

Bert's eyes lit up, but then he said, 'A little thing like you, making candyfloss?'

'Why not?' said Cassie. She saw Alex fidget, hopping from foot to foot, almost as if he wanted to be noticed. Of course! 'I won't be on my own,' she told Bert. 'You'll help too, won't you, Alex?'

A grin spread across Alex's face.

'All right then,' said Bert, 'but come and get me if you have any problems.'

Cassie grabbed Alex's hand and they raced to the candyfloss stall. Alex put

Comet down in the shade and looped his lead over a bollard. He filled a metal bowl with fresh water from the tap, and put it beside his puppy.

Behind the counter, Cassie looked at the whirring candyfloss machine, and the sugar heap, glistening like starlight. She looked at the growing queue of children. Then she looked again at the candyfloss machine.

'Alex,' she said, 'I've promised Bert I'll help, but – I don't know how!'

5
Going Up!

'What shall we do?' said Cassie.

'Let's see.' Alex peered at the machine. 'The heater warms the sugar . . . turns it into liquid . . . spins the liquid . . .'

'Excuse me!' called a girl's voice.

Cassie had to stretch to see over the candy-floss machine. A pretty girl with wavy fair hair and sky-blue eyes was second in the queue, and she tapped her foot impatiently. Cassie ducked down.

'It's Donna Fox,' she whispered to Alex.
'Her parents own Flashley Manor Hotel.
She's spoilt rotten.'

'Excuse *me*!' the voice said again.

Cassie stood on tiptoes. 'Hi, Donna,'
she said, doing her best to smile. 'The

candyfloss will be
ready soon.'

'I should hope
so!' said Donna. 'Are
you sure you know
what you're
doing?'

'I have an
expert here,'
said Cassie. She
bent down.

'That's you, Alex. Hurry up.'

'I won't wait forever,' Donna called. 'I'll buy my candyfloss somewhere else.'

I wish you would, Cassie thought, almost missing what Alex was saying.

'. . . Out come thousands of threads, and you twirl them on a stick,' he finished. 'Easy!'

Cassie poured sugar into the container in the middle of the machine, then Alex added pink food colouring. The container rattled and whirled, and out flew pale pink threads of spun sugar.

Cassie clapped her hands together and said, 'Well done, Alex! I knew you could get it working! Quick, pass me a stick before it overflows.'

Alex swiftly handed her one. Cassie twirled it round and round inside the bowl, and watched a pink cloud begin to form. When it was as big as her head, she stretched over the counter to pass it to the boy at the front of the queue.

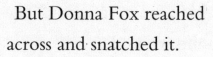

But Donna Fox reached across and snatched it. She flung her money on the counter and stalked away.

'Hey!' the boy shouted. 'That's mine.'

'Don't worry,' said Cassie, scooping up Donna's coins. 'I'll make an extra-big one for you.'

Alex was busy taking money and refilling the machine, so Cassie kept twirling spun sugar on to the sticks. But it was hard to reach the smaller children over the high bowl of the candyfloss machine. She glanced down. Her feet were hidden from view by sugar bags, so she thought about her bird charm. Silver sparkles danced around her bracelet, and her feet left the ground! She rose just high enough to reach both the machine and the children easily.

Alex opened a fresh bag of sugar and emptied it into the machine. He looked up at Cassie. 'You seem taller.'

'I'm on tiptoe,' said Cassie.

One little girl stood back from the others. Cassie thought she looked scared.

'Your turn, Rosie,' a tall girl said to her. 'Come on. The puppy won't hurt you.'

Alex called across the counter. 'Comet's very friendly.'

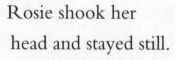

Rosie shook her head and stayed still.

'I know!' said Cassie. 'Let's make Rosie a special candyfloss. She'll have to be brave and go past Comet if she wants it. Put extra colouring in, Alex.'

He poured in double the usual amount. Soon Cassie was twirling a deep pink cloud of candyfloss. She held it out. 'Here, Rosie. It's rose-coloured to match your name!'

Was it her imagination, or did the candyfloss stick tug at her fingers, as if it was trying to break free?

Rosie's eyes widened. She took a deep breath, then edged past Comet to take the candyfloss. 'Thanks!'

Cassie smiled as she twirled another stick. Her plan had worked. But then she heard Rosie give a startled cry.

She looked up to see Rosie's candyfloss starting to rise. Up it went, taking the little girl with it!

'What's happening?' Rosie squealed.

'Alex, quick!'
cried Cassie.
They ran round
to where
Rosie bobbed
beneath her pink
candyfloss cloud.
Alex and Cassie each
grabbed one of her
dangling legs.

'There must be
a scientific reason
for this,' Alex
yelled, 'if I can just work it out.'

Cassie knew the reason. Tiny silver
sparkles danced all around the candyfloss.
They swirled down the stick and around

Rosie, then over Alex and Cassie too.
Somehow the charm's magic had spread!

Oh no, thought Cassie. *I'll have to be much
more careful with my magic.*

Aloud, Cassie cried, 'Pull Rosie
down!'

But they couldn't. Instead, they began
to rise too. As they floated past Comet,
the puppy jumped up and caught the hem
of Alex's jeans between his teeth. Up they
floated, bobbing gently in the breeze. Cassie
looked down to see the puppy's lead slide
off the top of the bollard.

'Comet's coming with us,' she called to
Alex, as silver sparkles swirled towards the
small white puppy. She looked up, hoping
Rosie wasn't too frightened, but the little

girl was busy trying to catch sparkles with her free hand.

Higher and higher they flew, the candyfloss at the top, then Rosie, with Cassie and Alex hanging on to her legs. Comet was last, gripping Alex's jeans in his mouth. And they were *all* surrounded by sparkly magic!

How on earth am I going to fix this? wondered Cassie.

6
Candyfloss and Clouds

Up they soared, until Astral-on-Sea looked like a tiny toy town below them. Even though it was daytime, Cassie could see the faint glimmer of stars and the pale silvery shimmer of the crescent moon.

She felt something brush past her hair – a fluffy blob of candyfloss had come loose.

Alex saw it too. First his eyes opened wide in surprise, then his mouth opened too. He leaned forward and took a bite.

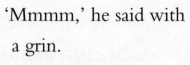

'Mmmm,' he said with a grin.

Cassie was too worried to smile back. She looked up. 'Are you OK, Rosie?'

But the face that looked down was smiling. 'This is fun!' squealed Rosie with delight.

'Look!' Alex pointed to a puffy white cloud scudding past. 'Flat bottom, bumpy top like cauliflower – it's a cumulus.'

Cassie sighed. Trust Alex to be studying the clouds when they should be trying to get back down to the beach!

The Best Friend Wish

Something white and fluffy drifted past
her nose. At first she thought it was a little
cloud, but then she saw the wagging tail.

'Comet!' she cried.

The puppy had let go of Alex's jeans
and now bobbed around Rosie. The little
girl giggled, then
reached out and
hugged him close.
'We're flying
together,' Cassie
heard her tell
Comet.

Hooray, thought
Cassie. *At least
Rosie isn't scared
of dogs any more!*

Alex was still cloud-spotting. 'That cumulus is evaporating,' he said. 'See? It's going wispy and disappearing.'

'The candyfloss is going wispy too,' said Cassie, feeling them all take a dip downward. Suddenly, she had an idea. 'Rosie – let's find out what your candyfloss tastes like!'

Rosie reached up and pulled away a handful of spun sugar. She popped it into her mouth. 'It tastes . . . magical!' she said. She tore off two more pieces and passed them down.

The Best Friend Wish

Cassie took a bite. The candyfloss melted on her tongue like sugary snowflakes.
Rosie pulled off more pieces for them all. As the candyfloss became smaller, the silver sparkles began to fade. They drifted down towards the beach.

My plan worked, thought Cassie happily.

Astral-on-Sea grew larger again, and soon they had all landed safely back on the sand.

Rosie hugged Cassie. 'Thanks!' she said. 'That was a lovely adventure.' She patted Comet. 'And thank you, Comet! I won't be scared of dogs any more if they're all as nice as you!'

A group of children gathered round.

'Rosie, you flew!' said a boy.

Before Rosie could speak, Alex said, 'It wasn't exactly flying, you know.'

'It looked like it,' said the tall girl.

'No, it's to do with changes in air pressure,' said Alex. 'Have you heard of thermals? Warm air expands, you see, and it rises . . .'

Cassie smiled. Thank goodness for Alex's scientific mind. He hadn't guessed there was magic in the air. The bracelet's secret was safe!

'I'd better get back to my mum,' said Rosie. 'Bye!' She'd only taken two steps when she bent to pick something up. It was a piece of hard, shiny driftwood, almost as round as a ball. 'This is for Comet to play with,' she said.

The puppy wagged his tail, and tried to take the wood in his mouth. It was too big, so he pushed it with his nose. The children laughed.

Bert walked up to the candyfloss stall,
leading Coco the donkey. 'Thank you for
helping me today, Cassie,' he said. 'Did you
have fun?'

'Oh, yes!' cried Cassie. She was relieved
that Bert hadn't spotted them flying
through the air! 'We've had a lovely
morning. Now it's time for us to go
home.'

Alex carried Comet's present, and the
three of them headed up the hill, back
towards Starwatcher Towers. Cassie
felt happy. She'd helped Bert with the
candyfloss and she'd helped Rosie get over
her fear of dogs.

Her heart skipped a beat. She'd
helped two people, hadn't she? Then

maybe . . . ?
She turned her
bracelet round.

There was no
new charm.

7
All Friends Together

'What's so interesting about that bracelet?' Alex asked. 'You keep looking at it.'

'It's hard to explain,' Cassie said. 'All I can say is that it's important for me to help people – like I helped Rosie not to be afraid of dogs.'

Alex frowned. 'What's the bracelet got to do with that?' he asked.

Cassie changed the subject. 'Look, we're home.' She opened the gate. 'Let's see if Mum's been baking.'

Alex unclipped the puppy's lead and dropped his driftwood ball. Comet's tail wagged madly. 'Yupp! Yupp!'

'He's scaring Twinkle!' said Cassie.

The cat arched his back, making his fur stand up like brush bristles.

Comet wasn't afraid. He nudged the driftwood ball with his nose. It rolled

towards Twinkle. When it stopped, the cat
reached out a paw to pat it.

'He likes it,' whispered Cassie.

Comet dashed forward and pushed the
ball again. This time Twinkle chased it and
batted it with his paw.

'They're playing,' said Cassie. 'I can't
believe it! Twinkle doesn't usually like
strangers.'

Alex watched the puppy and the cat
chase the ball around the garden. 'They're
not strangers any more – they're friends.'
He looked down, scuffing the grass with his
shoe. 'I wish I had a new friend too.'

Cassie remembered how she'd thought
Alex was unfriendly at first, but now she
knew he was just shy. She was about to

speak when it dawned on her – Alex had made a wish. And she was making it come true!

She grinned. 'You *have* got a new friend,' she said. 'Me!'

Alex looked up and gave Cassie an enormous smile.

'Wait there,' said Cassie. She went into the kitchen, where she found trays of freshly baked biscuits.

Cassie took two biscuits out to the garden. 'One for me, and the biggest one for you,' she said to Alex, 'to celebrate our friendship.'

A tingle ran up her arm.

'Huh?' Alex pointed to her wrist.

Her bracelet was glowing!

The Best Friend Wish

'Wow!' Cassie was overjoyed to see a new charm — a crescent moon! Its silvery shimmer reminded her of the real moon she'd seen as they flew among the clouds.

Alex's eyes widened. 'What's happening?' He peered at the bracelet, then at Cassie.

She decided to let Alex into her secret.

He was her friend after all. 'Sit down, and I'll tell you all about it. It's not science – it's magic!'

She explained about Stella Starkeeper, and how the charms were part of becoming a Lucky Star.

'They help me make wishes come true.' Cassie looked at her new charm. 'The bird charm gave me the power to fly, and we had such a brilliant time up in the clouds that now we're friends – and your wish came true!'

They nibbled their biscuits quietly for a moment, watching Comet and Twinkle play with the driftwood ball.

'So we really *were* flying?' said Alex.

'Yes, really.' Cassie smiled. 'It must be

hard for you
to believe in
magic.'

'Well, I'm
more used to
finding logical
explanations,'
he said.

Cassie nudged
him. 'Well, you can
use your super-scientific brain to help me
make the next person's wish come true.'

Twinkle was carefully licking Comet's
floppy ears clean.

'I'm really glad you and Comet are
staying at Starwatcher Towers,' said Cassie.

Alex grinned. 'Me too!'

Lucky Stars

★

Later, when Mum and Dad had kissed Cassie good night, she slipped out of bed and picked up Twinkle. She rose with him towards her glass ceiling and floated there, gazing at the stars. 'Who will make a wish next, Twinkle?' she wondered. 'And what power does my new moon charm have?'

As she drifted down to bed, the soft, clear voice of Stella Starkeeper floated across the twinkling sky. 'Good night, Lucky Star!'

Cassie's Things to Make and Do!

Join in the Lucky Stars fun!

The Best Friend Wish Wordsearch

I'm so glad that Alex came to stay at Starwatcher Towers, because now I have a new friend to help me make wishes come true. Can you be my friend and help me find the six friendship words hidden in this wordsearch? Remember, the words can go up, down, diagonally or backwards.

FRIENDS   SECRETS

SHARE   FUN

ADVENTURE   TRUST

E	R	T	Y	O	J	J	K	L
A	D	V	E	N	T	U	R	E
U	H	K	H	C	V	E	P	W
S	D	N	E	I	R	F	Z	O
E	S	D	F	R	F	C	A	T
C	A	S	D	F	F	A	Z	R
R	K	D	H	G	J	U	M	U
E	V	T	U	A	S	W	N	S
T	B	M	H	Q	R	Y	N	T
S	L	P	Q	I	U	E	H	O

Friendship Bracelets

Make an amazing friendship bracelet for all your bestest friends.

You need:
4 colours of embroidery thread
   about 80 cm long
Sellotape

Instructions:
Bunch your threads together and tie them in one knot about 3 cm from the top. Tape the knotted end to a table or the back of a chair. Separate the strands as shown.

1
2 3 4

1. Start with string 1 and loop it over and then under string 2. Hold string 2 straight, then pull the knot you've made tight.

1

2
3   4

2. Do step one a second time so you have made a double knot.

1

2

3

4

3. Now take string 1 and make double knots around each of the other strings (3 and 4).

4. Now do the same thing again. Start with string 2 and tie double knots, left to right, all the way across the other strings.

2

3   4   1

5. Keep going until the bracelet is as long as you would like it.

6. Gather all the strings together and tie a knot to secure them. Then trim the ends off.

Answers

Don't look unless
you're really stuck!

O	H	E	U	I	O	Q	P	L	S
T	N	A	B	M	H	O	R	Y	T
S	N	W	S	A	U	T	V	E	N
M	U	J	G	H	D	K	R	U	M
R	A	Z	A	F	D	S	A	C	A
T	A	C	F	R	D	S	E	S	C
O	Z	F	R	I	E	N	D	S	O
W	P	E	V	C	H	K	U	H	U
E	R	U	T	N	E	V	D	A	D
L	K	J	U	O	Y	T	R	E	E

The Best Friend Wish Wordsearch

Wishes really do come true

Lucky Stars

The Perfect Pony Wish

To read an exciting chapter,

please turn the page . . .

1
Stella Starkeeper

Cassie laughed as a star-patterned pillowcase blew off the washing line into her face.

'Wow! That wind's strong!' she said.

The two charms on her silver bracelet jangled as she pegged the pillowcase back on the line. She glanced at the charms – a tiny bird and a tiny crescent moon – and smiled. Their magic helped her to make special wishes come true.

I hope I meet someone with a wish today, she thought.

'When we offered to help your mum hang up the washing, I didn't expect to chase it round the garden!' called her friend, Alex.

Cassie's fair hair was blowing over her eyes. She pushed it away so she could see Alex collecting three socks that had blown into an apple tree. She laughed.

They started on the second washing basket.

The Perfect Pony Wish

'How many towels have you got?' asked Alex. 'I've already pegged out eight. That's about a third of what's here, so I calculate that . . .' He mumbled, frowning in concentration.

Cassie giggled. Alex loved maths and science, and was always trying to work things out.

'Remember, this is a B & B,' she said. 'That means ten times more towels than in an ordinary house.'

Starwatcher Towers was far from

ordinary. One part of it was the B & B and
the other part was an observatory where
Cassie's dad worked, watching the stars
and planets in the night sky. Even Cassie's
bedroom had a glass ceiling so she could lie
in bed watching the stars!

The Perfect Pony Wish

'You shouldn't really be helping,' said
Cassie. 'B & B guests don't normally hang
out their own towels.'

Alex shrugged. 'Mum and Dad are
meeting someone today, so it's good to
have something to do. Anyway,' he said
shyly, 'it's nice to help friends, isn't it?'

Cassie grinned. 'You bet!'

She hadn't been too sure about Alex
when he'd first arrived at Starwatcher
Towers. Then she realized he only seemed
unfriendly because he was shy, and they
soon became good pals.

The catflap clattered, and out popped
Alex's fluffy white puppy, Comet,
followed by Cassie's dear old cat, Twinkle.
Just as Cassie and Alex had become friends,

7

so had their pets.

Cassie stroked
Twinkle's
black fur.

'Meowwww,'
he yowled.

'Yupp!' barked Comet.

Cassie brushed her untidy hair out of her
eyes. 'You two should stay indoors,' she
told the animals. 'You might get blown
away!'

'Only if the wind's strong enough,' said

8

Alex, stroking his chin. 'I'll get
my anemometer,' he said, 'then I can
measure the wind speed.' He ran inside
and the wind banged the door shut behind
him.

Cassie threw another towel over the
line. As she pegged it down, she noticed
a bright light shining through the clouds
that scudded across the sky. *A star?* Cassie
thought. *In the morning?*

Dad had taught Cassie lots about the
stars. She knew that you couldn't usually
see them in the daytime because the sun is
too bright. As she watched carefully, the
star seemed to be swirling, whirling down
towards her!

Cassie remembered the last time she

saw a star behaving like that. Could it be . . . ?

With a *whoosh* and a *whizz* and a *fizz-fizz-fizz*, the star was beside her in a flurry of silver sparkles. It grew into a column of dazzling light. Then the light softened, and it changed into . . .

'Stella Starkeeper!' cried Cassie. 'You're back.'

A beautiful young woman stood before her in a short silver dress and a shiny silver jacket with star-shaped buttons. She wore glittery leggings and silver boots, and in her hand was a wand, tipped with a shining star. Her rippling hair fluttered in the wind, and on her head was a crown woven from strands of glistening silver.

Stella's velvety-blue eyes twinkled as they gazed into Cassie's brown ones. 'Hello, Cassie,' she said. 'I came to see how you're getting on with your new charm.'

The bracelet was Stella's gift to Cassie on her seventh birthday, a few days ago. She touched Cassie's bracelet with her wand, and a sprinkling of sparkles drifted to the grass.

'Never forget,' Stella said. 'You must listen for someone to make a special wish, then use the powers of the magic charms to

11

help make the wish come true. Then you'll earn a new magic charm.'

'When I earn seven charms, I'll be a real Lucky Star, just like you,' said Cassie.

Stella Starkeeper smiled. 'And you'll be able to grant wishes whenever you like!'

Cassie glanced at her bracelet. 'The bird charm gives me the power to fly,' she said, 'but what does my crescent-moon charm do? I don't feel any different. It does do something, doesn't it?' she asked.

Stella's eyes sparkled and her crown glittered as she leaned forward. 'Listen carefully, Cassie,' she whispered. 'Listen, and you'll hear something you never expected to hear.'

With a wave of her wand, Stella faded into a silvery mist. But a sudden gust blew her silver crown off!

'Wait!' cried Cassie.

It was too late.
Stella had disappeared.

13

Cassie chased after the crown as it tumbled over and over on the grass. She reached out to catch it, but it bounced against a tree and soared over the fence and down the hill.

She watched in despair as it disappeared from sight. *Oh no!* She'd never find it now!

'Got it!' yelled Alex.

Cassie turned. He was holding one of his science contraptions. 'Oh,' she said. 'Is that your amin . . . namen . . . ?'

Alex grinned. 'An-em-o-meter,' he said.

'Anen . . .' Cassie began. Then she laughed. 'Your wind-speed gadget!'

She watched Alex set it on the garden table. It had a stand with four arms, each

with a cup
shape at the
end. The wind
blew the cups
round and
round.

As Alex
pottered with
his measuring, Cassie remembered what
Stella had said. She wandered over to lean
against the plum tree's knobbly trunk. Then
she closed her eyes, thought about her
crescent-moon charm and listened.

A voice came from behind.

'This wind's blowing my coat all over
the place,' it said. 'I must look a complete
scruff.'

It was a weird, yowly sort of voice.
Cassie was sure she'd heard it before.

She opened
her eyes. It
definitely wasn't
Alex, but no
one else was
around. Only
Comet, who
was playing on
the other
side of the
garden. And

Twinkle, who was sitting beside Cassie,
staring up at her with his wide amber eyes.

Cassie gasped. '*Twinkle?*'

Lucky Stars
Wishes really do come true

Cassie is training to become a Lucky Star –
someone who can make wishes come true!
Follow her on more exciting adventures as
she meets new friends in need of help.

The Best Friend Wish

The Perfect Pony Wish

The Pop Singer Wish

The Birthday Wish

The Film Star Wish

The Ballerina Wish

The Christmas Wish

www.luckystarsbooks.co.uk